Arlo Had a Bad Day Today

Exploring Anxiety with Children

Words & Pictures by Sophie Kemp Cathcart

Having completed a degree in Primary Education at the University of Strathclyde in 2019, I have witnessed first-hand how big an issue mental health is increasingly becoming in children. Combining this with my own experiences in, and learning of, overcoming anxiety - and prompted by the evident effects of the 2020 pandemic - I decided to create this book as a tool for parents or teachers to use towards exploring the issue with children in a safe way. Through simple rhymes and friendly characters and pictures, this story will help children to understand some symptoms of anxiety, and what they should do in the case that they arise. Anxiety really can affect anyone, and early education is key to preventing it.

Leo was the **coolest** of cool guys.

He was the best kind of guy you could ever
meet; he was super clever (he always got
perfect scores in school tests), always kind,
and he was great at sports. He loved playing
music, he was **amazing** at video games,
and he was really confident too.

Nothing ever scared him.

But lately, something had started to feel not quite right for Leo. Sometimes, these days, he felt **nervous** when he didn't know why, and whereas before, he always felt happy, sometimes he now just wanted to **cry**.

But Leo was **cool**.

Cool guys don't cry, cool guys don't get scared, and cool guys **definitely** don't tell their parents when they don't feel cool anymore.

But there was someone Leo could tell. Someone he could tell **anything** to because he **knew** he wouldn't tell **anyone**.

Arlo.

Arlo was Leo's best friend. He used to do everything with him. One day a few years ago though, Mum and Dad told Leo that Arlo had to go because he wasn't **real**, and what Leo needed was **real** friends.

But Leo **knew** that Arlo wasn't pretend, and he knew that he was the **only** person that could help him just now.

4

"Oh Arlo, something's wrong with me,
I'm feeling scared and glum.
I never feel like myself anymore,
But cool guys don't cry to Mum."

...Arlo just blinked.

""That's it, Arlo!" cried Leo,
I know exactly what to do.
Instead of telling my Mum I need help,
I'll tell her I'm asking for you!"

The next day at school, Leo didn't have a great day. As soon as his Mum picked him up, his plan began.

"Mum? I need some help."

"Of course, Leo - what's the matter?"

"Oh, it's not for me Mum.
It's for my **friend**."

He said,

"Arlo had a bad day today,
He says he just doesn't feel right.
He said he had lots of
horrible dreams,
And didn't sleep much last
night.

He says he couldn't switch off his head, and he started to feel
really sad.
There were noisy voices taking all night,
That began to drive him quite mad."

"Oh," said Mum. "That doesn't sound very good. But tell Arlo not to worry - there's lots we can do to help him."

Mum told Leo that that night, they would have a nice, **relaxing bath** with Arlo. Then, they would have a **steamy hot chocolate** whilst listening to some **soft music** on the iPad, and Mum would would read them both a **happy story.**

She told Leo to tell Arlo that if he had trouble getting to sleep again, he should try to think of the **happiest day he can**.

He should imagine the things he would **see**,
the things he would **hear**,
the things he would
taste, and
the things
he would
smell.

Arlo liked that idea. He thought he might even try it **himself**.

Leo slept a little better that night, but the next day was still not good.

"Mum?" he said later. "We have another **problem.**"

"Arlo had a bad day today,
Everything was making him **worry,**
His heart was thumping really hard in
his chest,
The way it does when he's in a hurry.

He started to worry about you and Dad,
Thinking, "What if they are in **danger?**"
"What if Gran and Grandpa suddenly
get **sick**?",
"What if I'm approached by a stranger?""

"Oh," said Mum. "With not sleeping and starting to feel lots of worry, it sounds to me like Arlo is having some **anxiety**. But don't worry, there are things that we can do to help him."

Arlo didn't know what anxiety was, so Mum had to explain a little. She said that anxiety is a bit like a little man that sometimes comes into your head and makes you **worry** all the time. That scared Leo a bit, however Mum explained that the truth is, sometimes the little man **lies**. She said it isn't as clever as Leo or anyone that it visits; that it gets a bit **mixed up** sometimes.

Anxiety and the little man are really good at **tricking** people, she said.

It can say things that sound really real, when really, they aren't. She said the best thing for Arlo to do when this happens is to talk to an adult, because adults are really good at spotting when anxiety is playing tricks, and will be able to help him realise that what the little man is saying

isn't

true.

It made Leo feel better to know that the worries in his head were sometimes just tricks.

The next day though, things got worse.

"Mum? I need your advice again."

"Arlo had a bad day today,

His tummy feels all in a **knot**.

He didn't feel up to eating his lunch,

He isn't really eating a lot.

He says it's not just his tummy,

But his chest feels really strange too.

It's like there's a **big round lump** in

his throat,

AND he keeps needing the loo."

14

"Oh," said Mum. " I think that could be some more Anxiety. Anxiety doesn't just live in your head; sometimes it can play tricks on your whole body. But don't worry, there are things that we can do to help him."

Mum said that sometimes, anxiety can make you feel like you are **sick** when you aren't.

It can make you feel like there are **butterflies** in your tummy, or put you off your food.

It can make you all **sweaty** and give you a sore head...

...or it can even make you
feel like there is a
ball

    stuck

  in

      your

        throat.

She said that the most important thing to tell Arlo, though, was that he **isn't really sick**. It was just anxiety playing tricks again, so he shouldn't worry that there is anything wrong with him. She told Leo to tell Arlo that the next time he feels like this, he should try taking **10 big, deep breaths**. A walk in the fresh air might help too, she said.

Leo took note.

But still, the next day didn't go well.
"Mum? My friend is still having trouble."

"Arlo had a bad day today; he couldn't do his work in class.

He said he couldn't **concentrate** on anything,

And he finished all his tasks last.

He said it was like there was someone in his head,

Talking and distracting him all day.

The voices were running

as fast as a train,

And he couldn't make

them go away."

"Oh," said Mum. "This is definitely some more anxiety. But remember, there are **always** things we can do to help."

Mum said that is sounded like anxiety was up to its tricks again. She said sometimes the little man that visits people's heads can get a bit carried away. It starts to speak **really loudly,** and **really fast,** which can make it hard to concentrate on **anything.** But she told him to tell Arlo to remember that we can always make the little man **leave.** She said he should **tell an adult** when he feels like he can't concentrate, because he **won't be in trouble** and the adult will be able to help him concentrate again.

This made Leo feel **happier.**

But it did not make the next day much better.

"Mum? Can I ask you about something again?"

"Arlo had a bad day today,

The voices in his head were back.

This time they were telling him **horrible** things,

It felt like he was **under attack**.

They told him he wasn't as important as his friends,

That he would always **disappoint** you and Dad.

They said he wasn't a good enough person,

No words were good, only **bad**."

"Oh," said Mum. "Anxiety is at it again! Remember though, Arlo shouldn't worry because we can always do things to help."

She said the most important thing to remember is that the little man in your head sometimes tells l i e s.
Even if the little man says that Arlo isn't doing well in his schoolwork, Mum said that he should always remember that he knows for a fact that he is.

If the little man says, "You are going to do **rubbish** at this game!", Arlo should say, "I know that I'm **really good** at this."

If the little man says, "Your friends **don't like you!**", Arlo should say, "I know that I am a **really good friend.**"

Leo liked this advice - the little man sometimes tells lies. That night, standing in front of the mirror, he talked about lots of things that he likes about himself.

He pictured the little man starting to leave his head.

The next day, Leo was feeling much better. That's why what happened surprised him so much.

"Mum?" he cried, "I nee- I mean, Arlo needs your help."

"Arlo had a bad day today - really, especially bad.
One minute he was happy doing his work,
The next he was crying like mad.

His heart starting racing in his chest,
His hands were shaking and sweaty.
It suddenly got really hard to breathe,
And the room looked all fuzzy and unsteady."

"Oh," said Mum, bringing Leo in for a cuddle, "It sounds like Arlo had a panic attack. They can be really scary, so I'm not surprised he was so upset. But remember, there are always things we can do to help."

She said that panic attacks can be really frightening because it can feel like you are in real danger and that your body is shutting down. She told Leo to tell Arlo, though, that he doesn't need to worry because he is never really in danger - it's just another anxiety trick. She said that, as always, he should tell an adult if he thinks this is starting to happen. An adult will be able to help calm him down, she said, by doing things like taking deep breaths, cuddling a fluffy toy, or talking about things that he can see, hear and smell.

Leo **smiled** at his Mum.

"I'm really proud of you telling me about how Arlo has been feeling, Leo. He should **never be embarrassed** to talk about things like this, and he won't ever be in trouble. I think that if he hadn't told you about his Bad Days, he would only have started to get worse and **worse.**

You should **never bottle things up**.

Do you think that if he starts to feel these things again, you will tell me **right away?**"

"Yes, Mum," smiled Leo.

"I'm not - oh, I mean, Arlo's not - scared of anxiety anymore. He knows that there is **nothing wrong with him** and he knows that there are always things to do to **help** with the little tricks that anxiety and the little man sometimes play."

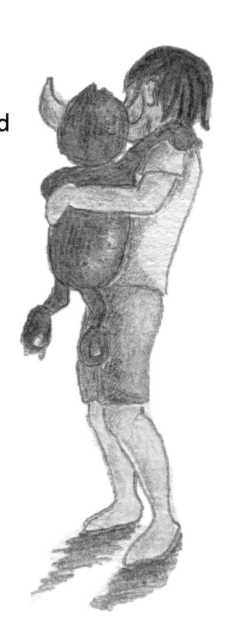

28

From that day on, Leo's Bad Days started to get **less** and less,

and less

and less.

Arlo smiled.

Things to discuss with your child:

1. Why did Leo not want to tell his Mum about how he was feeling?

2. What would you have done if you were Leo? Do you think it was a good idea that he pretended to be asking about Arlo instead of telling the truth?

3. Have you ever felt any of the things Leo talked about?

4. What would you do if you started to feel worried and not yourself anymore?

Key things to remind your child frequently:

1. If you get anxiety, it doesn't mean there is something wrong with you. You haven't done anything wrong.

2. Lots of people get anxiety - it's very normal.

3. We can always do things to help the anxiety go away.

4. The little man in our head that anxiety causes sometimes tells lies. We always know better than the little man.

5. The most important thing you can do is to always tell an adult how you are feeling.

Keep smiling.

Printed in Great Britain
by Amazon

57461067R00026